One Page Conversations, Vol. 1

Some Funky (and Brief) Conversations and Some Funky (and Digital) Art

By
Bill Holtsnider

Art

In addition to the text, I have created all of the art in this book. Please my gallery at **bill-holtsnider.pixels.com** to see the art on canvas prints, posters, throw pillows, shower curtains, t-shirts, and almost every other sort of thing.

Bio

Bill is a writer and graphic artist living in Boulder, CO. He has lived many places around the country and the world but prefers the people, the landscape and climate of Colorado to anywhere else.

Conversations and Art

1. A bet made while shopping for a computer

"Is not."

"Is so. 186,000 miles per second is the fastest anything can travel."

"You made that number up. You pulled it out of your—"

"Look, bozo. I did not pull that number out of anything, except my seventh grade science textbook three years ago."

"I still think you invented it."

"Not only did I not invent it, lots of other people know this number, too."

"As if."

Berk smiled a little, then looked around the store slowly. He was looking for one particular type of person and he was sure they were in this store somewhere. If they were anywhere, they were in their mother's basement or here, shopping in this used computer store.

Then Berk spotted her.

"I'll make you a bet," Berk said casually to his friend.

"No, I'm not betting with you. I always lose. Always. One of my GameBoy controllers is actually yours because I lost a bet. Most of my Magic cards are yours because I lost—"

"Whatever," Berk said suddenly. "Listen, I will bet you lunch that I can walk up to that girl with glasses in the red dress, ask her one question, and get her to say '186,000 miles per second.'"

"Ha! You couldn't get her to say 'Leave me alone you slimebag.' We betting lunch? Let's put a cap of twenty bucks on this, so when I lose—which somehow always happens—I don't end up taking you to your uncle's bistro and dropping all my cash."

"Lunch for two for twenty bucks it is."

Berk walked over two aisles with Camber following close behind.

"Excuse me, miss," Berk said, smiling widely, "my friend and I forgot the exact number and you looked like a woman who would know. Do you know the speed of light?"

"186,000 miles per second," she replied, smiling. The guy talking is kind of cute, she thought, but the other one is too preppy-looking...

All That Lux (ArtBloq: Photos, PhotoArt)

All That Lux

(bill-holtsnider.pixels.com/featured/allthatlux-bill-holtsnider.html)

2. Two guys chatting about mates at the diner

"Are you carrying?"

"I'm packing, if that is what you mean. I am always packing. I was born packing. I am so packed—"

"No, that is NOT what I mean."

"Are you talking about that other love of my life?"

"Yes. That other love of your life, the one you don't have. I have a method to find your soul mate."

"Sole mate? The only one for me? I have a method to find my POLE mate, but not my soul mate."

"Pole mate? What's that? Never mind—I know what it is."

"A woman I want to see dance on the pole for me. The, ah, stripper pole. Yeah, that's it, the stripper pole."

"My concept is a little more advanced spiritually than your 'Pole Mate.'"

"Oh, another one of your high-falutin' ideas, eh? Got any room in the concept for some ice-cold beer?"

"No, no beer and no stripper poles. Just true love. The truest love between two humans."

"Oh, okay, I'll buy some of that. How much does it cost? No, wait, let me guess—nothing down and only $24.99 for thirty six months. Satisfaction guaranteed or your heartbreak back."

"No, it is not a layaway plan. It's—never mind. I don't know why I discuss these things with you anyway."

"It must be my charming personality."

"Yeah, that's it. And the fact that you seldom shower—that's a plus, too."

"I drive a rig, for crying out loud. Some trucks have beds but not that many have showers."

"Whatever. Don't you want to find out how to meet the woman of your dreams?"

"I already know how to do that. That's what trucker cafes are for. Sit at the counter and ten minutes later some hottie comes over to offer you a chance to party."

"As wonderful and healthy as that sounds, I mean something a little more, uh, elevated."

Flower Splash (ArtBloq: Photos, PhotoArt)

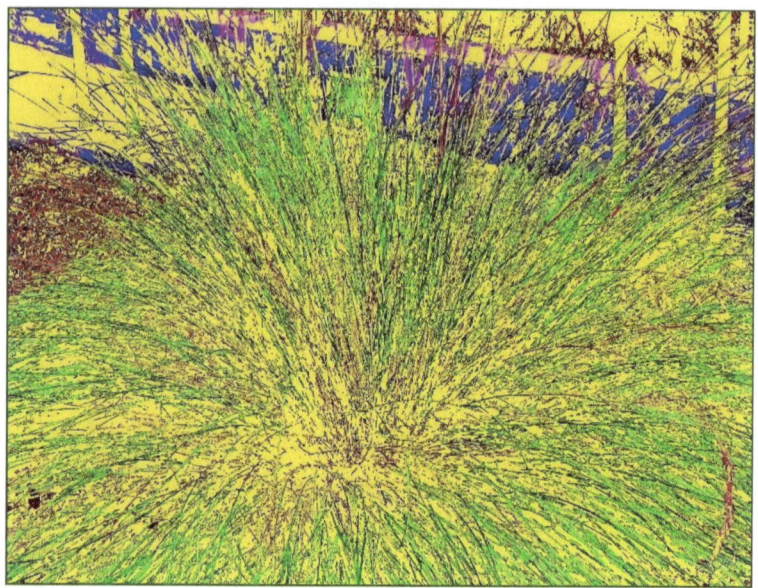

Flower Splash

(bill-holtsnider.pixels.com/featured/flowersplash-bill-holtsnider.html)

3. Outside (and inside) the cafe

"Biome? What in the hell is a biome?" asked Deek.

"We all got one, pal," said Bobby

"Don't 'pal' me, pal. And I just got checked for all that last week and I am clean."

"It is not a thing to check *for*—it is a thing you have and need to keep healthy. It is a part of your body—"

"You're not going to get all sciencey on me, are you?"

"Talking about body parts is getting sciencey?"

"Yeah it is. It's gross. Next you'll be telling me that bacteria is good for you."

"Some are, actually."

"See! See! I told you."

"See what? Some bacteria eat other bacteria. If they didn't, you'd die."

"Whatever. You're grossing me out with all these 'facts' and stuff," said Deek. "I'm trying to order lunch, dude."

"You brought it up."

"Yeah, well now I am bringing it down."

They both laughed. It was the third day of a seven-day ride through upper New York. Bobby and Deek had gone on a week-long trip every year since high school.

"I'm bringing it down to this restaurant. And what I am going to eat for lunch. Is that too theoretical for you?" said

Deek.

"No, I'm good. Us sciencey types eat lunch, too."

"That's good. Do you sciencey types eat hot dogs?"

"I wouldn't go that far."

"With onions? And hot sauce?"

"Hardly."

"And ice cold beer?"

"Craft beer? Yeah, I would like some craft beer. Or maybe an IPA."

"I got your IPA right here, pal."

"IPA, VA, whatever. Speaking of the VA Hospital, Deek, I've got something to tell you."

"Oh, no. The VA. Do we have to? You know I hate that place and anything to do with it."

"Well, you're gonna hate this news, then. But this is the last time I'll make this trip."

"What! Why?"

"I just got the diagnosis yesterday. My biome is under-performing, to say the least. Which is bad."

"Have you tried Jerry's Salvage Yard? Maybe you could get a used biome there."

"Anything The Savage would sell me would kill my microbiome faster than eating a hot dog..."

Runs Like It (ArtBloq: Photos, PhotoArt)

Runs Like It

(bill-holtsnider.pixels.com/featured/runs-like-it-bill-holtsnider.html)

4. Two ladies having lunch at the country club

"So when did she get it done?"

"How should I know?"

"You're her sister, for God's sake. If you don't know, who does?"

"No one, as far as I can tell. The doctor who did the work probably doesn't even know."

They both laughed.

"You'd think she was a celebrity or something the way she skulks around, keeping secrets that have secrets."

"Yeah, I've known her my whole life and I know twice as much about you as I do about her."

"Well, it's not like you and I just met."

"No, but I have known you 'only' since college. I've known her since she was born."

The waiter came by and they ordered a second round of drinks. It was Tuesday at the club and no one was at the restaurant. Well, no one of any importance, that is. There were people at the club, but Terri and Jinnie saw no one they needed to have seen them.

"Are you going to ask her?"

"Ask her what?"

"Ask her if she got a new polo pony. Of course not, you idiot—are you going to ask her when she had her work done?"

"No, I am not going to ask her. She wouldn't tell me anyway. I don't even know if she is married or not."

"She's been living with that guy for years … Ricardo. What difference does it make whether she is or not?"

"She didn't even tell her own sister that she's married? That's cold."

"Well, I don't have a sister, period. Cold or not. So you are lucky in that regard."

"I don't really have one either, in any way that counts."

"If your mother was alive she would hate you for saying that."

"She would hate me for saying it, but she would also understand why I said it. Liz was as cold to Mom as she was to me."

"Something must have happened to her back in the day."

"Yeah, it did. She was born."

Steps Down (ArtBloq: Photos, PhotoArt)

Steps Down

(bill-holtsnider.pixels.com/featured/steps-down-bill-holtsnider.html)

5. The morning of the birthday party

"Are you going to tell me what the surprise is?"

"No. Then it wouldn't be a surprise, would it?"

"It would be when you first told me."

"Uh, well, yes, that is technically true, but actually false."

"What does that mean?"

"It means I am tired of talking about this and I don't want to talk about your birthday gift anymore. If you want to know the truth, I didn't even want to get you a birthday gift. Dad made me do it."

"He did not."

"He did so."

"You don't do anything you don't want to do and you never do anything he says to do, so I don't believe you anyway."

"Well, whether you believe me or not is not pertinent."

"Pertinent? Pertinent! When did you become so legal-sounding? You don't even know what 'pertinent' means."

"I do so."

"Fine, Ms. Smarter-than-the-average-smart-phone, use it in a sentence."

"I just did. And for your information, Ms. 411, your criticisms of my vocabulary are not deleterious to my person."

"'Deleterious!' Ha! What is all this stupid fancy talk?"

"I have decided to be a lawyer. I am going to law school

when I graduate from college."

"HA! First you have to graduate from high school, then you have to gra—"

"I know all that. But first I have to give you your birthday gift. I have to get that pain out of the way and then I can get on with my very important schooling."

"Giving me a birthday gift is that much trouble for you?"

"Yes it is. It is a gratuitous dissolution of my extremely meritorious time. So once I give you the goldfish and the bowl and the water, I am done."

"A fish?! A goldfish! Gross! Who thought that was a good idea for a gift for me?"

"What would you prefer—a new calculus book?"

sunset2 (ArtBloq: Photos, PhotoArt)

sunset2

(bill-holtsnider.pixels.com/featured/sunset2-bill-holtsnider.html)

6. On the top of the cliff before the dive

"Fine, fine, let's do it. If you want to do it, let's do it."

"I don't want to do it unless you want to."

"I want to, I want to."

"You sure?"

"Do I have to beg? Five minutes ago YOU didn't want to and now you want to. Let's just go."

"It is a long way down."

"Not really. But it is getting longer while we stand here."

"No, it's not."

"Yes it is, you big baby. Do I have to remind you whose idea it was to climb up here and jump off in the first place? This is pretty much the last place I would volunteer to spend an afternoon of my vacation. I would pay to see other bozos leap off this stupidly high rock but I would never think of doing it myself. I would never even climb up this high, much less dive off it into the freezing cold water."

"It isn't that high and the water is not freezing."

"It IS that high and I am sure the water IS freezing. I don't need to dive in to make sure."

"Look, I bet Dan we would both dive off and if we don't we owe him beers for a year."

"You idiot! YOU will owe him beers for a year. I didn't make that bet—you made it behind my back."

"Whatever. You owe me from the last time we played golf."

"When was that—1997?"

"No, that was last month and you know it was. So you owe me."

"I owe you beers, I don't owe you a plunge to my death into the icy cold waters of the Artic."

"First of all, this is Mexico. In the summertime. Secondly, this is the jump off cliff for tourists. It is maybe 30 feet. There are community pools with high dives higher than this."

"Not in any community pool I've ever been to."

"That's because the only swimming pools you've ever been to are the kiddie pools your mother put up for you in the backyard."

"Ouch. OK, fine, fine, let's do it. Stop whining and jump."

"I will if you will."

"What do think I am doing up here on top of this rock? Put up or shut up."

Red and Purple (ArtBloq: Graphics)

Red and Purple

[*(bill-holtsnider.pixels.com/featured/red-and-purple-bill-holtsnider.html)*](bill-holtsnider.pixels.com/featured/red-and-purple-bill-holtsnider.html)

7. The three of them at the bank, late at night

"Do you have a plan?"

"If I had a plan, we wouldn't need you, would we?"

"That's not true. In any case, I am a *city* planner, as you know. What we are doing here is not city planning."

"City planning, country planning, global planning, global warming. I don't care about all that—I just want the money."

"Yes, we all just want the money, but I suspect they will not just hand it over to us if we ask them."

"Maybe if we ask nicely," she said softly. The two men turned to her. They had forgotten she was there.

"That is an idea," the first guy said to her slowly. "Not a very good one, but it is an idea." The men sniggered. "We have to find a way to get this money and we should have thought of a way to do that waaaaay, waaay before this."

She was nonplussed. "Look, all we need to do is explain to them that this is our money and we want it back."

The taller one looked at her for a long time—maybe five seconds—before he spoke. She felt the force of his beady eyes staring down at her.

"They are not just going to hand the money over to us. No one just hands over money."

"The federal government does," she said, just to say something back at him. She was squirming under his gaze.

"These people are not the federal government," he replied. "They aren't the local government. They aren't even the local mob. This is a ruthless gang of killers that would end your life faster than you could say 'Hello, my name is Linda. Can I have the $245 you took from us on the subway please?'"

"'Ruthless killers' is a bit strong," the other man said. "They are punks, but I don't think they are killers."

"And how do you know that? Have you asked them? Because I don't think she has asked them and I know I haven't asked them, so have *you* asked them?"

"Just because they have green hair highlights doesn't mean they are killers."

"No, but they are not button-down corporate types, either."

Like 'Em? (ArtBloq: Graphics)

Like 'Em?

(bill-holtsnider.pixels.com/featured/like-em-bill-holtsnider.html)

8. On the bus going to prison

"When I said 'Let's go to the joint,' I didn't mean—"

"I know what you meant, you meathead. You meant 'Let's go find some chicks at that dancing place we went to before.'"

"Yeah, that is what I meant."

"Well, now we ain't going to that joint, we are going to The Joint."

"And we ain't smoking no joint on the way, neither."

"Either."

"What?"

"You shouldda said 'either.'"

"I shouldda gone with Tony last night, that's what I shouldda done. When you said you—"

"I know, I know—you shouldda, couldda, wouldda."

"All I know is, I wanted to go out and party and you said you knew a place."

"I did know a place."

"You knew a place to rob."

"Well, we needed some money, didn't we? You can't party without money."

"Yeah, but I didn't know—"

"There are a lotta things you don't know."

"I know not to use firearms in a holdup."

"Listen, Dope—"

"Don't call me that!"

"Listen, Daniel Dopelmiester—if that is your actual, real life name—"

"It is."

"Listen, Daniel, you are goin' to the big house with me and twenty-eight of your new best friends. All of us are chained to the seats and this bus ain't stopping at no McDonalds. I am very hungry, so if you don't mind, please stop telling me how you are innocent."

"I never said I was innocent."

"SHUT UP!"

Everyone looked at the two men. Since they were in the front row, up on the left, no turning was required.

Explosion7 (ArtBloq: Graphics)

Explosion7

(bill-holtsnider.pixels.com/featured/explosion7-bill-holtsnider.html)

9. On the Space Station

"I have no idea when he is coming. We just talked to him last week on the ground and he said he would be here tomorrow."

"If he said he'll be here Friday, he'll be here Friday. I'm sure of it."

"How can you be so sure?"

"How can I be so sure? I texted him, that's how."

"You texted him? I didn't know we could—"

"We can't, you idiot. I was joking. We're out in space, for crying out loud! But try and listen to me. When the Commander says he is coming, he's coming. He is a standup guy. Unlike you, I might add."

"Ouch. Why would you say something like that?"

"Like what?"

"That I am not a standup guy."

"Well, you're not."

"Yes I am."

"No, you are not. I'll give you a perfect example. You haven't paid me back the money you owe me, for example."

"The twenty I borrowed last year at the bar? That measly twenty?"

"Yeah, that measly twenty."

"Wow. You're not kidding, are you? You are pissed at me

because I didn't pay you back twenty bucks I borrowed when I was down."

"That's your idea of being down? Needing money to buy a woman a drink at a bar?"

"Not just any woman—that was my perfect future wife."

"Ha! She must be with your ten other perfect future wives now, cuz she left as soon as she sucked her free-to-her cosmo down."

"Well, she COULD have been my future wife."

"Yeah, and she could have been pretty, too, but she was neither."

Lake & Clouds (ArtBloq: Graphics)

Lake & Clouds

(bill-holtsnider.pixels.com/featured/lake-and-clouds-bill-holtsnider.html)

10. Who sits where?

"Well, what do you mean, exactly?"

"You know exactly what I mean."

"I do, but I don't want to go there, so I am giving you a way out."

"Thank you, but no thank you."

"What does that mean?"

"It means exactly what you think it means. I think we should go ahead with the original plan."

"You only think that because you came up with the original plan."

"That's true, I did. I thought it was a good idea then, and I think it is a good idea now. I think we should go ahead and try it."

"Okay, you're the boss."

"Am not."

"Are too."

"If I am the boss then you would have to do EXACTLY what I say."

"Well, uh—"

"That's what I thought. You want me to be the boss when hard decisions need to get made, but you don't want me to be the boss when we're cruising around, looking for a place to eat lunch or deciding who sits where."

"Is this about trying to get me to sit next to Marla? Because I've already told you, I am not doing that."

"As if."

"What does THAT mean?"

"It means if I decide you are sitting next to Marla, you are sitting next to Marla."

"You are not the boss of me."

"Hmmm ... how quickly they flip."

Turning Somewhere (ArtBloq: Graphics)

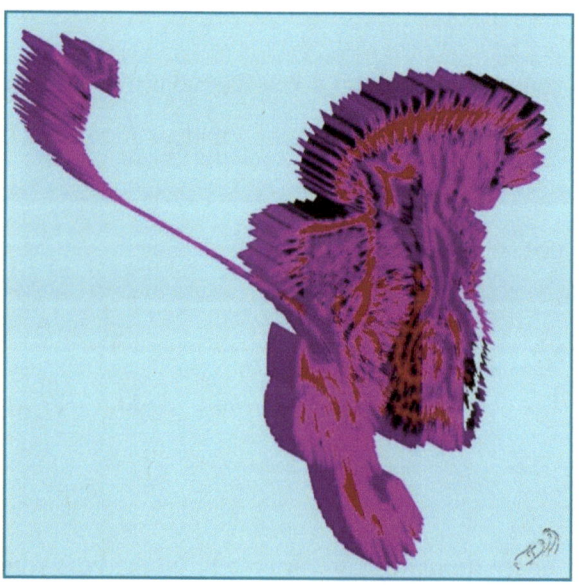

Turning Somewhere

[(bill-holtsnider.pixels.com/featured/turning-somewhere-bill-holtsnider.html)](bill-holtsnider.pixels.com/featured/turning-somewhere-bill-holtsnider.html)

11. Watching the two of them buying a used car

"So we are buying this one even though I hate the damn thing?"

"Watch your language."

"You are bothered by 'damn'? Good thing you don't hear me around my friends."

Two salesmen watched them bicker from the other side of the lot.

"How much are we betting that they don't walk out of here with the car?" said one salesman to the other.

"It's Murph's sale. He's hanging back, standing a few feet away, trying to be far enough away but crowding them. He's hoverin' like a mother hen."

"Hey, that's a good nickname for him: 'Mother Hen.'"

The two of them laughed a little too loudly and the three people in the lot looked over at them.

"Nice. If we keep this up we'll cost Murph his sale," said the other salesman out of the other side of his mouth.

"His first sale of the week."

"His first sale of the month."

"Yeah, well, it has been slow for all of us this month. Blizzards keep casual buyers away. They stay at home, they don't go out and look at used cars."

"Whining again?"

"No, I am not whining. I am just saying—weather affects car sales."

"And I am just saying that if you are whining about the weather, you are whining."

"Whatever. I went to the Vikings game last Sunday."

"You did?! You dog. You saw them beat—"

Suddenly they heard a profanity-laced scream and the wife stormed off the lot. The husband stood next to the car, looking sheepishly at the ground.

"I told you yesterday when he first came in by himself," the first salesman said, "one leggers never buy."

"One leg, three legs, eight legs—with this weather you gotta go for every chance you get."

As he said that, a beautiful woman walked in with her boyfriend/fiancé/husband/male-neighbor-to-help-buy-a-car-guy.

"Speaking of three legs," said the second salesman...

Wall Art1 (ArtBloq: Graphics)

Wall Art1

(bill-holtsnider.pixels.com/featured/wall-art1-bill-holtsnider.html)

12. On the surfboard (two kids, one board)

"When are you going to start helping?"

"When are you going to steer us to where we can catch a big wave?"

"Listen, bozo, you're only on this board cuz your brother tricked me into taking you out. If it wasn't for me, you'd be shining seashells for tourists back at the shop."

"And if it wasn't for me, you'd be in jail right now, becoming a large cellmate's new best friend."

"Yeah, that was yesterday. This is today. Paddle."

"Like I told Simm yesterday, I do whatever I want. And I don't feel like paddling right now."

With that, Tor tipped the board. Caught off guard, Rimmy tumbled into the water, but not before dramatically throwing his arms into the air for maximum affect.

"You did that on purpose!" he sputtered as he came up for air.

"Oops. Sorry about that," Tor said, suppressing a smile, "a wave came up."

"I'm gonna report you, you big idiot, if you don't take me out to a wave and—"

"Fine, fine. Get back on. I'll take you to a big wave."

Rimmy climbed back on the board. He sat up and said "Go!" in his strongest 13-year old voice.

Tor could tell by Rimmy's tight grip on the board that the boy was scared. And he knew the kid had no idea how to ride a big wave. But he enjoyed the thought of him eating all that sand when the waves sent his pummeled white body back to the beach after they caught his precious big wave.

"C'mon," Tor said to his board mate, "let's go for the REALLY big waves."

"Yes! This is what I have been waiting for my whole life!"

As if, thought Tor to himself.

If only I had looked to my left, he thought, I would have seen that little punk watching me. I saw the store camera and I was watching the cashier, but I didn't see the little twerp sulking in the corner.

It was only a six-pack, but it would have been his third conviction in six months. This little surf town took "crime" very seriously and he knew from talking to his friends that even shoplifting, to say nothing of shoplifting beer, was considered an "offense punishable by jail time."

It turned out the juvenile was the cashier's—and shop owner's—little brother. The cops were not called, but Tor had to agree to take the kid out paddling 'to a big wave' every day for six days—one day for each beer. If only he had tried to lift a single Slim Jim...

coyote1 (ArtBloq: Drawings)

coyote1

(bill-holtsnider.pixels.com/featured/coyote1-bill-holtsnider.html)

13. Captain! Captain!

"And?"

"And what?"

"That's it? That's your whole story?"

"Yes, that is my whole story. What do you want—nuclear explosions and car chases and violent, nighttime stabbings?"

"Well, yeah, actually, I do want some of that. Something a little more exciting than 'We met, we fell in love, we water-skied in Cancun, we married, we divorced, end of movie."

"Well, I am sorry, Mr. CaptainAmericaMan, but not all of us can lead superhero lives."

"I don't lead a superhero life, I just do more than sit around in my underwear and watch TV all day."

"First of all, I don't sit around in my underwear. I am fully clothed."

"Well, that is a relief."

"Secondly, I don't watch TV on a 'television set' like you do. I stream shows on my Xbox."

"Oh, that makes a BIG difference. You watch TV on your video game console."

"Yeah, what's so weird about that?"

"Nothing weird, just supremely, disgustingly, lazy and pitiful. And pathetic. Pathetic, too."

"What is so pitiful about a life full of games, TV shows, and movies?"

"Do you have wireless headphones, too?"

"As a matter of fact, I do."

"And full speed streaming capabilities?"

"Of course."

"You have all this hardware and all this software. Got any goals? Or are any other humans involved?"

"I don't need other humans."

"Of course you don't."

"She's gone, dude, and she ain't coming back—according to her. My plan is to burrow in and survive the winter."

"The winter, spring, summer, fall—your plan is to burrow in forever."

"Well, yes. As soon as I find my shot glass, I'll be fine."

"As soon as you find your Shot Glass of Self Pity, you'll be fine..."

Chair in the Waiting Room (ArtBloq: Drawings)

Chair in the Waiting Room

(bill-holtsnider.pixels.com/featured/chair-in-the-waiting-room-bill-holtsnider.html)

14. On the school bus the first day of sophomore year in high school

"So, who do you think we'll get for homeroom this year?"

"Mr. Stinkle."

"'Mr. Stinky'? No way."

"Yes way."

"You are secretly in love with him."

"I am not. YOU are secretly in love with him."

"I am not. He's a guy, for one thing."

Razz smiled. "Just cuz you're a guy doesn't mean you don't like guys," she said.

"Yes it does."

"No, it doesn't. My cousin Dirk is a guy and he likes guys. He told me so himself."

"Well, I am not your cousin Dorky and I do not like guys. I like girls. Pretty girls like you."

"And I like you, too. A lot. But don't you think it's strange that you never once hit on me?"

"Hit on you? Why would I do that?"

"Every other guy in school does. Why don't you?"

"You are my friend. I am not going to hit on you."

"Exactly."

"Exactly what?"

"Every guy in school—including some of the teachers, by

the way—every guy wants to be my 'friend.' They all want to 'get to know me better.' But you don't."

"I already know you. You already are my friend."

"Yes, we are friends. Close friends. Maybe best friends." She looked away when she said that.

He looked at her more closely. "But?" he said, expectantly.

"And maybe best friends tell each other everything. And maybe best friends tell each other things other people are scared to talk about."

"I guess. You have something to tell me?"

"I do. I mean, I could, but you might not like it."

"I like everything you say."

"Yeah, well, you might not like this thing."

"Just say it already!"

Forest1 (ArtBloq: Drawings)

Forest1

15. A complicated bedtime reading one night

"And then there is the afterlife."

"Again? Do we have to, Dad?"

"Yes we have to. This is an important topic. "

"Yeah, it must be important—you have told me about it every night this week. And every night last week. And every night back from, like, when it happened."

"I do not talk about it all the time."

"Yes you do."

"No, I do not."

"Look, Dad, I know you care about this dying thing a lot, but can we talk about something else for once?"

"Like what?"

"My friends get read lots of fun books by their parents at night. Marcia's parents are reading the Harry Potter books to her. Terk's family is reading some books about exploring other planets."

"Those things have the afterlife in them."

"Whatever. Just because a book has dying in it, does not mean the whole book is about dying."

"For a seven-year-old, you are one smart cookie."

"For an old guy, you are not that smart, Dad."

"Ouch. Why do you say that?"

"Cuz. You don't ever listen to me, you just talk. You talk

about yourself and your office and your job and—"

"OK, OK—I get it. I should listen to you more. Tell me—what do you want to say?"

"Well, for one thing, please don't talk about dying anymore."

"You already said that. And why don't you want to talk about it, anyway? We all die eventua—"

"Stop it. I don't care if we all die. Right now I am not dead, I am alive. Mom isn't alive anymore, but I am, and my friends are, and you are, so let's talk about being alive, not being dead."

"OK, sweetie, you are right. Let's talk about being alive."

"And another thing."

"Yes."

"Let's talk about when I can have some of that ice cream you promised me yesterday."

Fish5 & candle chakra (ArtBloq: Drawings)

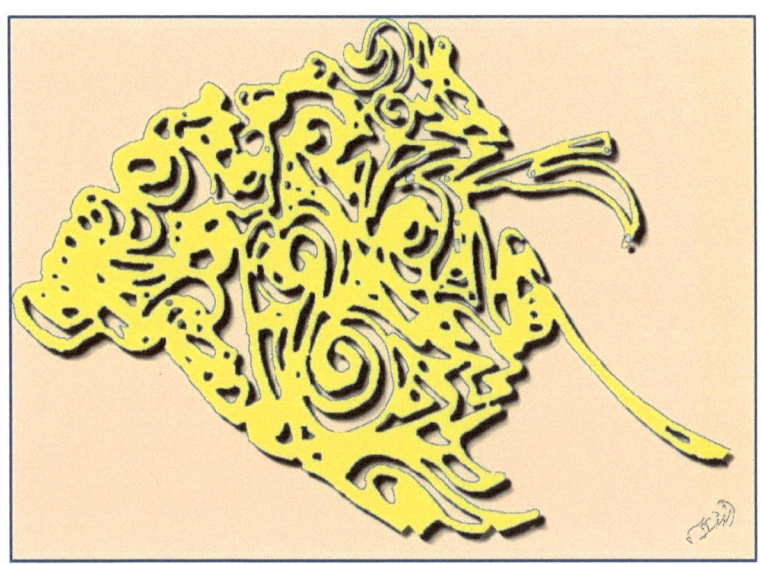

Fish5

(bill-holtsnider.pixels.com/featured/fish5-bill-holtsnider.html)

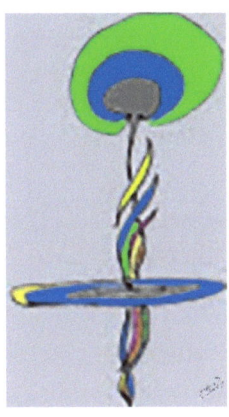

candle chakra.jpg

(bill-holtsnider.pixels.com/featured/candle-chankra-bill-holtsnider.html)

16. Father/son talk

"Hw r u?"

"I'm fine, I guess. Why are you talking like that?"

"AFAIK, I am talking normally."

"No you are not."

"Yes I am. How am I talking?"

"Like an autorobotothingy."

"?"

"Dad, Dad, Dad. Sometimes you talk like a Dad. Just like a Dad."

"Because I am one?"

"Just cuz you are one don't mean you gotta sound like one."

The dad sighed. "Well, Mr. RobotPersonMan, I think it is important for you—"

"This oughta be good."

"I think it is important for you to, uh—"

"Yes, what is it so important that I do? Clean up my room? Bring back the lifesavers I shoplifted from Jerry's Shack last week? Tell Donna I do love her, even though I don't and never have, and just said that to get her to—"

"NO. No. None of that. I think it is important that you tell me why you are back here."

"Back at the house?"

"Yes."

"Instead of what?"

"Instead of running away."

"Because of what I did that night?"

"Yes, because of what you did that night."

"I didn't actually do it, you know."

"All I know is three people claim they saw you do it and the cops believe you did it. They think you stole that car and they're looking for you right now. Why they haven't already shown up here is anybody's guess."

"It might be because they know I have hated my parents' guts since like forever and I would never go back to their house in case I saw them there."

"Well, there's that..."

Clouds3136 (ArtBloq: Clouds, CloudArt)

Clouds3136

(bill-holtsnider.pixels.com/featured/clouds3136-bill-holtsnider.html)

17. On the Space Shuttle (2)

"Where have you been?"

"I am here. Where are you?"

"'I am here, where are you?'"

"I am right here. I have been here for 188 days. Where have you been—walking the dog?"

"Not exac—Wait, you're right, I was walking the dog. In outer space. I wanted Krypto to see an exoplanet before he goes to Doggie Heaven."

"Wait, Krypto is going to Doggie Heaven?"

"Yes, someday we must all pass."

"Well, I got news for you, my friend. I ain't going to Doggie Heaven."

"Says he who is closer to Doggie Heaven than any canine or canine owner on Earth."

"I am not on Earth and I am not going to Doggie Heaven. Those are two facts I know."

"As far as I can tell, those are the only two facts you know."

"Very funny. I have been up here for half a year waiting for somebody else to show up and they send a bozo like you. Do you have a real function or did you come all this way just to insult me?"

"Most people—not you, of course, but most people—can do more than one thing at a time. I came here to abuse you, yes, but I also have some work to do on my ship. I have jobs I need to do."

"Like what?"

"Like bring you news."

"News? I get the news every day, every minute. Have you ever been near a spaceship before?"

"We don't call them 'spaceships' anymore. We call them 'Aerodrone React Command Ships.' 'ARCS' for those of you who can't spell."

"ARCS actually stands for 'Any Remaining Capsults Send,' by the way. You can make stuff up, but you can't actually DO anything. That would be you—a remaining capsult."

"I don't know what a 'capsult' is, but if it is related to an insult, you are not very good at it."

From back at base, Scott watched the lines of code scroll down before him on the monitor. Space travel was nothing like he had expected, despite all the years of training. But this—a dialogue between two spaceships? Nothing in his entire life had prepared him for this.

Clouds 378 (unretouched) (ArtBloq: Clouds, CloudArt)

Clouds 378 (unretouched)

[(bill-holtsnider.pixels.com/featured/clouds378-unretouched-bill-holtsnider.html)](bill-holtsnider.pixels.com/featured/clouds378-unretouched-bill-holtsnider.html)

18. Family Calculus

"Let's start at step one. Your father met your mother on a boat."

"Yes."

"They had sex, conceived you, and never spoke to each other again."

"Yes."

"Your mother married Gitaro, who owned seven horses."

"Yes."

"Gitaro also had two daughters from a previous marriage, one of whom married the niece of Liberace's personal valet."

"Yes."

"The other daughter married Gitaro's cousin—never mind, I can't do this. It is too complicated. I can't keep track."

"What are you talking about? You are The Professor! You understand calculus, for crying out loud. You teach the stuff. The rest of us can't even spell it."

"I understand *Newtonian* calculus. Not *Family* calculus. Family Calculus is too complicated for me."

Don and Mitch were sitting on lawn chairs, sipping beers, bobbing with the gentle rock of Don's houseboat. The boat listed a bit, the chairs were worn and did some listing of their own, and the men were "working" (a term that repelled both of them) to acquire the same state of listinglessness in their minds.

They practiced acquiring this listinglessness every Sunday morning. The two women in their lives went to services (presumably to pray for the men's salvation) while the two men went to the houseboat. One group was trying to go northward, the other drifting southward. Metaphorically speaking, of course.

Don was older, clearly over 50 but probably not yet 60. Mitch was a little younger. Both had goatees and were wearing their "Sunday worst," ratty jeans and plaid shirts that had seen better days. The boat had a dress code: "If you look nice, you can't come aboard." Both adhered strictly to the code.

Mitch wore a "CAT" baseball cap. Don knew this was an affectation, since Mitch wouldn't know how to find the engine in his BMW, much less how to drive a tractor.

Don was more complicated. He had military service, three ex-wives, and children all over the globe.

Despite their differences, Don and Mitch were close friends. They had been 'swapping lies of life and loves' for a long time. If friendship is pretending to believe the other person's obvious dishonesties, then these two were deep pals.

"So what you are saying, oh wise one, is that there is a limit to your understanding?"

They both laughed.

"I exponentially have no idea what you're talking about when you launch into family and kid stuff."

"Cuz you have a null fac—"

"Enough! I am very smart but very clueless, okay. I can draw graphs of space and time folding but I can't change a diaper."

This conversation is excerpted from my book of short stories called "*Some Rivers Run*." It will be published in 2017.

Grey Clouds1 (ArtBloq: Clouds, CloudArt)

Grey Clouds1

(bill-holtsnider.pixels.com/featured/grey-clouds1-bill-holtsnider.html)

19. A man and a woman on Friday night in a hotel bar near the office

"I keep wanting to call you 'Loreola.' It rhymes with—"

"I know what it rhymes with. And it is not my name. Not even close."

"It is close."

"It is not. My name is 'Loreli.' There is no 'a' or 'ae' or any other weird letters you want to put into it."

"Speaking of putting things into—"

Loreli recoiled. "Do you turn everything into a conversation about sex?"

"Don't you?"

"No, I don't. And neither do any of my friends."

"Well, all of my friends do. My name, by the way, is Marko."

"Marko, it is clear all of your friends must be immature, adolescent boys."

"And all your friends must be stuck up girls."

"My girlfriends are women who have giant paychecks, not giant compensatory watches."

"Your friends have giant compensatory purses for the boyfriends they don't have."

"YOU are never going to have a girlfriend, that's for sure."

"Yes I am, but you are not going to be the lucky one."

"I AM going to be lucky if it's not going to be me."

"If I had enough breath, I would say 'Ouch.' But I am breathless with excitement."

"What are you so excited about, I hate to ask?"

"You leaving for the airport to catch your next flight to Toronto."

"Toronto? Ha! I am not going anywhere. I just arrived in sunny LA two weeks ago. I moved here from Minneapolis. I report to my new boss on Monday."

Marko smiled, looked down at his glass, and asked, "What is your new boss's name?"

"Gordon. Gordon Marchessi. Not that you would care. Not that you would know him. He would never hang around low-lifes like you."

"As a matter of fact, I do know him."

"You do not. "

"Nice to meet you, Loreli P. Sullivan. My name is Gordon Marchossi. My friends call me 'Marko.' Hope you like the cold."

With that, Marko stood up, put a twenty-dollar bill on the bar, and walked out.

The Light Behind (unretouched) (ArtBloq: Clouds, CloudArt)

The Light Behind

(bill-holtsnider.pixels.com/featured/the-light-behind-bill-holtsnider.html)

20.At the discussion about the lack of a will

"For what?"

"For crying out loud! You are giving me my share of the ranch."

"As if. I put more work into that place than anyone else. Certainly more than you did."

"You have got to be kidding."

"I'm not kidding. I am totally serious."

"We'll see how serious you are after we talk to my lawyer."

"OUR lawyer, bucko. Don't you forget that. She is OUR lawyer. And I am sure that when you talk to her she is going to ask you who put the most time into the place. Who kept it up? Who traveled icy roads in January to check the pipes hadn't frozen? Who shoveled the snow off the roof after the blizzards? Who fed the cattle when Jake was sick for a week?"

"First of all, you went there two or three times all of last winter—"

"Five, actually."

"Whatever. Five. You no more climbed on the roof of that house than I ran a marathon last month."

"You said you ran the whole thing."

"No, I said I ran the 5K they had the day before. You weren't listening."

"Well, you aren't listening to me, either. That place is all mine."

"Secondly," he said with exasperation, "secondly, you wouldn't know how to feed the cattle any more than you would know how to ride an elephant."

"I have ridden an elephant, for your information, Sparky."

"I'm not talking the pink elephants you see when you are on one of your sprees."

"I haven't done that for a long time."

"You haven't done very much of anything for a long time."

"Well, I have done something, and that is more than you, my friend."

"'Brother.' I am sure you meant to say 'my brother.'"

"What I meant to say was 'You have done diddly for maintaining this ranch so I am getting it all, *brother*.'"

"And what I am saying—I don't *mean* to say this, I am *actually* saying it—is what you *want* don't mean diddly. What it says in the will is what matters…"

Grey Clouds2 (ArtBloq: Clouds, CloudArt)

Grey Clouds2

(bill-holtsnider.pixels.com/featured/grey-clouds2-bill-holtsnider.html)

21. On the bus going to prison

"Hey, man, what are you in for?"

"You must be new."

"Why do you say that?"

"Nobody asks anybody that question in here."

"Well, I ain't anybody. I'm somebody."

"You ain't nobody."

"You should have said 'You are not somebody.'"

"Huh?"

"You said two negatives. 'I am not a nobody.' But I'm actually somebody."

"Even if you are the king of this bus, you're a nobody."

"I ain't nobody."

"Even if you keep saying that, you aren't nobody."

"You are right about that. I *am* a somebody."

"You can twist words around all you want. We're all going to the same place."

"Yes, heaven."

"Uh, in my case, probably not. Probably that other place, the hotter one. But whatever. I was talking about something else. We're all going to The Big House."

"Yeah, well, your definition of the Big House and mine are two different things."

"Do you have any idea what is going to happen to you next?

I guess not, since you have a big grin on your face."

"I am smiling because you and I disagree that we are all going to the same place, although we are calling it the same name, The Big House. We'll get to where *you* think we are going much sooner than where *I* think we are going."

"Whatever that means. I hope where you think we are going takes in people wearing orange jump suits."

"Oh, clothes, facial hair, money, fame—none of that matters. We all get in."

"Hmmm. Sounds great. Do they let nobodies in?"

"All bodies and nobodies are welcome."

"Then since you ain't a nobody, you should have no problem..."

Tunnels2 (ArtBloq: Clouds, CloudArt)

Tunnels2

(bill-holtsnider.pixels.com/featured/tunnels2-bill-holtsnider.html)

22.Snakes in the tunnel (maybe)

"I'm not going in there."

"Yes you are."

"No I am not."

"You agreed to help me."

"This is not helping you. This is going down into depths of hell."

"Or under the highway, one or the other. I am not sure which."

"I vote 'depths of hell.'"

"I vote you the scarediest guy in this county."

"Is that even a thing?"

"What, 'county'? Oh, that's right, you guys call it a 'parish.' I didn't grow up here like you did so I forget you all live in churches."

"*Parishes*, we all live in parishes here in Louisiana, not churches. You Yankee boys wouldn't understand."

"You're right. You watch 500 miles of left turns on Memorial Day, kill frogs for fun, and live in churches. I don't get any of it. But luckily, I don't have to get it. I just have to get out of here alive. And you promised to help me."

"I will. I am. You want to get outta this swamp alive, do not go through that tunnel."

"Well, I sure as hell am not staying here."

"Why not?"

"They'll find me, for one thing. And there are snakes here. We just saw one, and where there's one snake, there's a whole pack of snakes."

"Well, you are right about that. There are snakes everywhere, even on the other side of that tunnel."

"How do you know that? Have you ever been over there?"

"Well, no, not exactly. But there are snakes everywhere, all over the entire US of A, as a matter of fact."

"No, not in New York, there aren't. Not in Manhattan. There are no snakes in Manhattan."

"Ha! There are more snakes per square inch in that little city than the entire state of Louisiana."

"First of all, Manhattan is not 'little.' It is 24 square miles—"

"Never mind. You're big, I get it. You have lots and lots of people in your city. Your whole state probably has more people than our whole state."

"Yes we do."

"Yeah, and you got more snakes, too. We have the kind that slither and bite you on the ankle. You got the kind that walk on two feet, carry briefcases, and bite you in the net worth. Or bite you in the stock portfolio. At least with our types, you can generally get your health back."

"Generally. Not always, but generally."

"With your types, you ain't never getting your money back."

"No, you are not. I am living proof of that."

BlottoBlot Nanomapling (ArtBloq: Nanomaplings)

BlottoBlot

(bill-holtsnider.pixels.com/featured/blottoblot-bill-holtsnider.html)

23. Two grave diggers at work

"If not now, when?"

"I hate that phrase."

"Whether you hate it or love it, the question remains. Speaking of remains."

"Please. You are definitely new at this. We don't make jokes about graves, jokes about dead bodies—"

"YOU don't. But I do."

"Whatever. Can you stay on topic for one minute?"

"I don't feel like staying on topic."

"Well, I don't feel like digging that grave, either. But I'm gonna do it. It's my job."

"Aren't you the noble one."

"Not noble, just employed. By the Man. For a long time. And I intend to keep it that way by continuing to do what I am told to do."

"You do everything you are told to do?"

"By my boss, yes. By everyone else, no."

"No wonder you can't stay married."

"Whatever. I am going to finish this job."

"By yourself."

"Yes, by myself."

"I already told you I'll help."

"Thanks, but no thanks."

"What, don't you think a woman can dig a grave?"

"I am SURE women can dig graves. I have been buried by more women than I can count."

"You just told me grave diggers don't make grave jokes."

"Not to each other they don't. But to the general population they do."

"I am not in the general population."

"Yes you are. Your HUSBAND was a grave digger, but that doesn't make you one."

"Well, my husband is dead now, so I am all you have. You want help or not?"

"Help burying my best friend from his 5-foot widow?""

"5-foot, 3 inches, I'll have you know."

"Whatever."

NotCandidatable Nanomapling (ArtBloq: Nanomaplings)

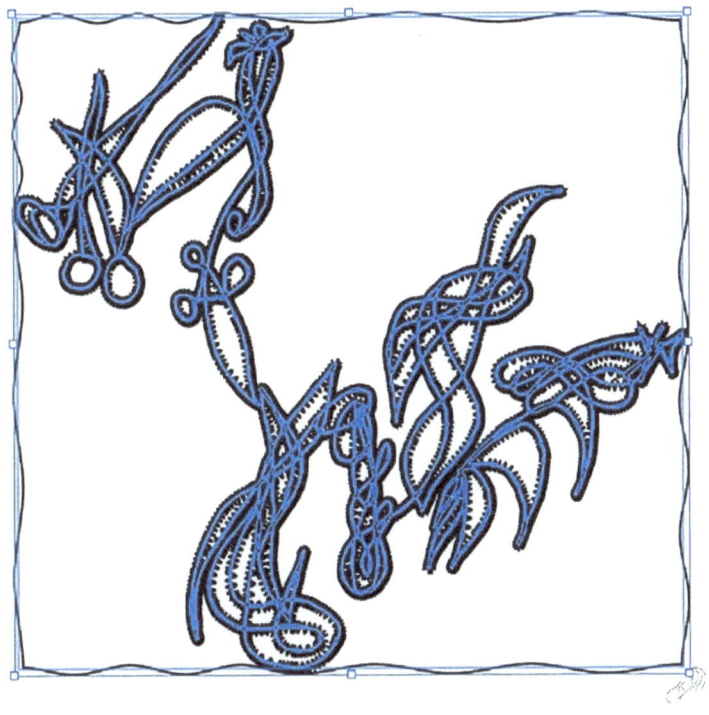

NotCandidatable Nanomapling

[(bill-holtsnider.pixels.com/featured/notcandidatable-nanomapling-bill-holtsnider.html)](bill-holtsnider.pixels.com/featured/notcandidatable-nanomapling-bill-holtsnider.html)

24. Not going back, no way, no how

"When do you plan on going back?"

"Never."

"Hmmm. 'Never' is a long time."

"Longer than any other time."

"Well, it is not longer than 'never and one minute,' but it is a long—"

"Can you be serious for one minute?"

"I am serious. You are never going back to see your family. I get that. I don't think it is a good idea to say 'never' but if that's the way you—"

"That is the way I want it. That's the way it is. I don't want to explain to my grandmother why I beat up that old man."

"I don't blame you there. I wouldn't want to have to explain that either."

"I had to do it. If I hadn't, he would have attacked me."

"Whatever."

"Those are the facts. No feelings were involved."

"Hmm. Well, I disagree on that point."

"What does 'Ms. Never-plus-one-minute' disagree with? Which fact is up for dispute?"

"Well, for one thing, I disagree with the whole 'no feelings were involved' idea."

"What do you mean?"

"I mean, you told everyone—me, the cops, Terry—that you had never seen that guy before."

"I hadn't. Don't you believe me?"

Maria paused before answering. "Terry and I both saw your face when that guy appeared at the picnic table."

"He does not work for our company. I did not want some random stranger stealing our food. Those were Nathan's hot dogs we had flown in from New York."

"We now have over 100 people working for the company. Do you still know every single person who works here? I know you *used to*, but do you still?"

"I am the CEO. It is part of my job to know every employee."

"Is it? Is it part of your job to beat up old guys in the park, too?"

"OK, OK, he was not just a random old guy."

"What a surprise."

"He wanted money."

"So do I—but you don't beat me up. Granted, I am the VP of HR, so if you DID beat—"

"He's a loan broker. Well, kind of a loan broker kind of guy. He wanted the money I borrowed from him last year."

"You borrowed money from a loan shark?"

"I had to. The company was floundering and I knew if we could hang on for a few more months, we could make it. The big deal with those guys in Dallas—"

"Which fell through."

"Which fell through, you're right, but other big deals came through and we came out of the slide."

"But you had to get dirty money to make it happen."

"Yes..."

Cascadal7 (ArtBloq: Nanomaplings)

Cascadal7

(bill-holtsnider.pixels.com/featured/cascadal7-bill-holtsnider.html)

25.On the plane/in the bed/on the phone just before the jump

"When I said no, I meant NO."

"Marjorie, what you should have said is 'I really, really, don't want to, Ron.'"

"I really, really, really don't want to, Ronald."

"Are you sure?"

"Are you listening to me?! I said I don't want to do it."

"OK, but you know they don't give refunds."

"I know. I thought I wanted to but it turns out I don't. I have a bad feeling about this."

"Yes, well, I'm guessing that bad feeling is pretty common up here every the time to jump out of the airplane gets near—"

"NO!"

"OK, OK. I'll go out with my instructor and see you later on the ground. But you know I am never going to let you live this down. After all, it was your idea in the first place to get us all up here. 'Let's go skydiving as a team-building exercise!' Skydiving with a bunch of programmers…"

"Yeah, I can't believe I said that."

"What I can't believe is you got fifteen people up here and YOU were the one who chickened out. YOU were the one who bailed."

"Do you have to tell everyone?"

"Are you kidding? They are all watching us from the ground. They have already jumped. They are waiting for us 'management types' – that is what they call us – to make our jump."

"Well, they are not going to be rewarded. I have no intention of jumping out of this plane."

"That's funny, when we tried to get you to change the company's IRA contribution policy, you said the same thing."

"You're bringing that up now?! When we get down on land—"

"IF we get down on land."

"WHEN we get back down on land. Stop scaring me like that. In fact, when we get back to the office you can just collect your things and don't bother coming back."

"Wow. Fired at 10,000 feet. My friends will be jealous. If you ever get back on land, give me a call."

"No way, Jose."

"You go through CTOs like hot knives go through melting butter. You'll be calling me."

Dancin'1 (ArtBloq: Nanomaplings)

Dancin'1

(bill-holtsnider.pixels.com/featured/dancin-bill-holtsnider.html)

26. All that spikin'

"Well, do you like my red spiky hair?"

"Yes."

"Do you like my spiky red dog, Spike?"

"Yes."

"Do you like spicy red curry?"

"Yes, a lot."

"Do you like Stephen Curry?"

"Yes, a lot."

"Do you like me?"

"No, not really."

"Because?"

"Because you ask too many stupid questions."

"No I don't."

"Yes you do."

"Like when?"

"Like right now."

"I am not asking stupid questions."

"Yes you are."

"Name one question I have asked you today."

"If the Empire State building drove across the country, would it fit going across the Golden Gate Bridge?"

"Oh, that. Well, I did ask you that."

"And about three thousand other stupid questions, too. But

why do you care about the Empire State Building, anyway? You are from Lincoln, Nebraska, you live in Lincoln, Nebraska, your entire family is from—"

"I know, I know. I am a Nebraskan through and through. Just like you are a New Yorker through and through. You love hot dogs, loud noises, lots of humans, weird foreign food, talking about the stock market all the time, and some other things I can't think of right now."

"Yes, and despite all that, I love your spiky hair."

"It is great, isn't it?

Not a Fish and Arrows8 (ArtBloq: Nanomaplings)

Not a Fish

(bill-holtsnider.pixels.com/featured/not-a-fish-bill-holtsnider.html)

Arrows8

(bill-holtsnider.pixels.com/featured/arrows8-bill-holtsnider.html)

27. Two girlfriends outside the science classroom. Waaay outside.

"I need your gravity assist."

"Where did YOU hear THAT term?"

"I heard it on a news item about the planet Jupiter."

"You don't even know what it means."

"Yes I do."

"No you don't."

"I need your assistance in using gravity. Isn't that what it means, Mrs. Science-Lab-Queen-of-the-Petri-dishes?"

"Well, yes, that is *technically* what it—"

"'Technically?!' 'Technically?' The girl who wears her pocket protector clipped to her bra—"

"I do not!"

"Look, just give me a boost up, OK? I'll climb over the wall, sneak into the classroom through the window, grab the final term papers—"

"LOOK at the final papers! No grabbing. Only looking at the papers."

"OK, fine, I'll just look at the papers. But if my grade is less than a D—"

"Which it probably is."

"Which it probably is, then I am going to have to do something."

"Do something?! Like what? You told me we would break in to see what our grades were before the long weekend. You didn't say anything about changing anything."

"Why do you think I brought this?" Jeane reached down, pulled something out of the front pocket of her jeans, and presented it to Margie with pride.

Margie's jaw dropped. Jeane was holding a red pen in her hand. It was exactly the kind of red pen Mr. Somethers used to mark their lab reports with.

"I will NOT be a part of this! You said we would only LOOK, not CHANGE, the grades on our papers."

"Do you think I came out here to this grungy old field at midnight to break into the high school to just LOOK at my final paper?"

"Why not? That's why I came."

"You came to find out if you got an 'A' or an 'A-.' You came out to see if you can go for Early Decision on your application to college. I came out to see if I have to repeat this year, because I know I am flunking Math and if I flunk Science, too, I won't have enough credits to graduate."

"You tricked me. If I knew you were going to get us arrested—"

"Arrested?! For changing a grade? Girl, if they are going to arrest us, it will be for 'B&E'—that's what my dad calls Breaking and Entering."

"I know, I know—you tell us at least once a week your father is on the police force."

"And you tell everybody once a week how to your father left you and your mother—"

"Look, do you want a boost up or not?"

"Touchy, touchy. I need a boost alright. And I could use some of that alimony money your mother is getting from her rich ex-husband, too. That is a boost I could really use."

"Well, don't hold your breath. That woman barely gives me lunch money, much less extra money for clothes and stuff."

"And yet you guys live in a big-ass house in the Heights? What do you have—six bedrooms? For two people and a cat?"

"Two cats, actually."

"Oh, TWO cats. That makes ALL the difference…"

Shella4 (ArtBloq: Nanomaplings)

Shella4

(bill-holtsnider.pixels.com/featured/shella4-bill-holtsnider.html)

28.Two tween friends

"I have invented a new type of technology."

"As if. *You* have invented an entirely new technology. By yourself. Overnight."

"No, not overnight. But yes, by myself."

"Well, that is just 'brilliant,' as your loser cousin 'Barry the Nit' would say."

"Barry the Brit."

"Brit, Nit—what difference does it make? He's gone back to Mother England now, so we have the rest of the summer to ourselves."

"Why do you hate him so much? He's a nice kid."

"First of all, I do not hate him. I despise him intently, but I do not hate him. I save my hatred for Mr. Caruthers who sent me to the principal's office—"

"I know, I know, three times last week. You have told me this story 40 times already."

"Well, I'm sorry. But that guy is such a jerk. And second of all, Barry is not a nice kid."

"Is so."

"Is not."

"I assume you have proof that will stand up when I take this case to the Supreme Court for defaming my cousin and calling him a 'slimebag.'"

"I did not call him that, but it is certainly an appropriate name for him."

"Because—"

"Because he hit on my sister, for one thing!"

"Your sister is 10 years old. Barry is eleven. I am not sure there was all that much hitting on going on. Maybe some hitting EACH OTHER, but I doubt there was any hitting ON."

"I knew you'd take his side!"

"I'm not taking his side. I just think your statement is ridiculous."

"Fine. Go ask my sister—she'll tell you."

"I'm sure she will. That girl will say anything to anybody if she thinks it will cause them pain."

"That is a hurtful thing to say."

"Keep her away from my parents. Five minutes with her and they'll think I belong in prison."

"For the record, I think you belong in prison, too."

"Now what did I do?"

"It is more what you did NOT do that matters."

Key7 (ArtBloq: Nanomaplings)

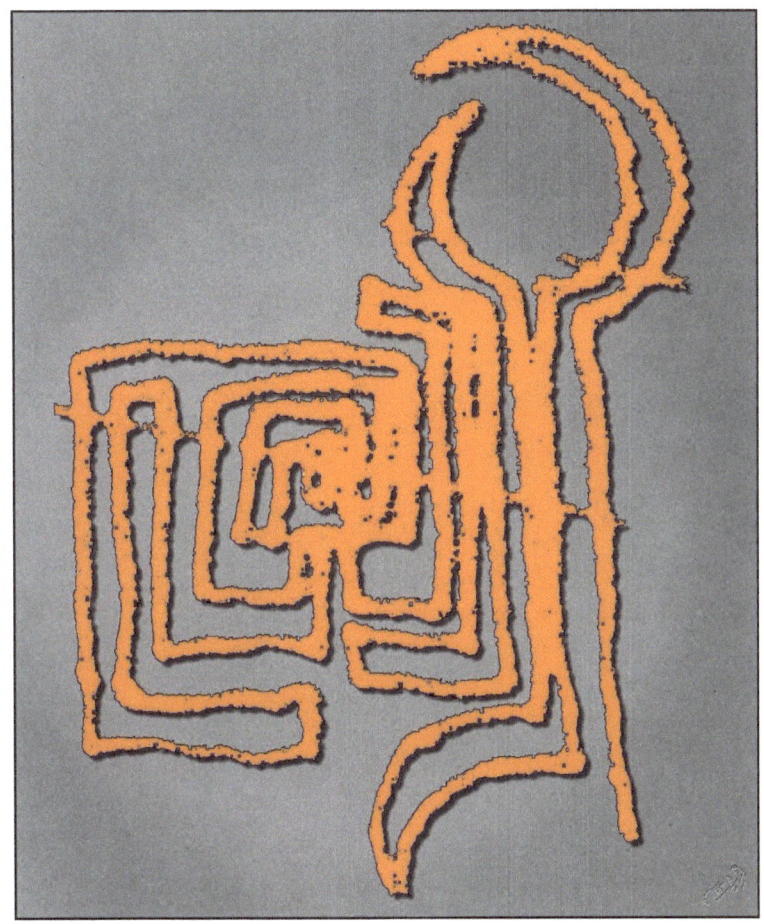

Key7

(bill-holtsnider.pixels.com/featured/key7-bill-holtsnider.html)

29. Two guys on the park bench talking physics

"Let's talk quantum physics."

"Let's talk salary caps instead."

"Aren't you EVER serious?"

"Salary caps ARE serious. Quantum physics is not."

"As if. Quantum physics helps the world directly in many ways, including the development of an atomic clock."

"Salary caps are much more important than that. If a team has no 'cap room' or too much 'dead money,' their chances for a great season are poor."

"You are—how can I say this politely?—a complete idiot."

"Thank you, sir. But I fear that is just the beer talking."

"Whatever do you mean? I have only had—let me count the bottles here—1,2,3,4,5,6,7,8—eight beers! So let's talk quantum mechanics. Or salary caps, either one. They are actually the same thing."

"Another reason I do not want to talk quantum physics or quantum mechanics with you is because you don't understand it. You are drunk now, so you REALLY don't understand it, but in general, even when you are sober—which is rare, by the way— you spout on about things you don't understand."

"Quantum physics is only a theory, by the way."

"Well, that is a good example of what you think you know, but actually you don't know. Quantum physics is not a theory, it is not an unproven theory, it is a FACT. A scientifically proven fact."

"Well, salary caps are a theory, I know that."

"No, salary caps are not theories, either. And since you've had so much alcohol, I think it is time for us to discuss how you are getting home."

"How I am getting home? I am driving my car to my house, of course."

"As if. You are so drunk you think your car is a theory."

"Well, it is. Actually, the CAR is not the theory, the LOCATION of said car is a theory. Schrödinger and all that. That damn Schrödinger! If he had not fried his cat in his oven, I could find my car."

"That is not actually what happened, but never mind. I'll call Uber."

"I don't need a ride from some stranger."

"Yes you do. You're drunk."

"That's only your theory."

"No, that's a fact, too."

The Pointing Tree (ArtBloq: Trees, TreeArt)

the Pointing Tree

[(bill-holtsnider.pixels.com/featured/the-pointing-tree-bill-holtsnider.html)](bill-holtsnider.pixels.com/featured/the-pointing-tree-bill-holtsnider.html)

30. Likin'/Lovin'

"I am the one who thought of the idea of Batman getting married."

"As if."

"No, really, I did. He already had a cape and a car and a cave and a cool belt and—"

"I know all that. I watch every Batman movie. I read Batman fan fiction. I read the online comics every week, dude. I have read the comic since I was ten."

"Yeah, I know, but did you know he could have a wife?"

"He's already had several wives, actually."

"What? With weddings and all that?"

"Why do you suddenly care about this? You don't know the difference between a Marvel character and a DC one. Why are you suddenly comic-geeking out on me?"

"I am not geeking out on you."

"Yes you are. Tell your sister you invented a wife for Batman and see what she says."

"OK, maybe I am geeking out a little, but I still thought of the idea."

"An idea that has been had by 6 or 7 trillion other comic book readers, animated TV show watchers, and movie fans, by the way."

"Oh. Well, what about Superman? I think he needs a wife."

"I think YOU need a LIFE!"

"What is that supposed to mean?"

"It means your superhero plots are moronic. Sophomoric. Ridiculous. Shallow. Common."

"Hmmm. But besides all that, do you like them?"

"No, and I don't like you, either."

Bez is shocked. After a few seconds, between tears, she said, "But you said you loved me a few days ago."

"I do love you. I don't like you."

"What does that mean?"

"It means that one can love a person—generally one HAS to love a person, there is no choice in the matter—but not LIKE the person, there is SOME choice involved here, though not a lot."

"That is really deep. And stupid. Did you read all that in a book?"

"I have read a book or two, if you must know, but when I talk about liking and loving, I am speaking from experience."

Floridian Row1 (ArtBloq: Trees, TreeArt)

Floridian Row1

[*(bill-holtsnider.pixels.com/featured/floridian-row-bill-holtsnider.html)*](bill-holtsnider.pixels.com/featured/floridian-row-bill-holtsnider.html)

31. On the train, fleeing

"We are never gonna live this down."

"No, we're not."

"Maybe if we don't say anything—"

"As if. That doesn't matter. Everyone knows."

"Not everyone."

"Everyone. Trust me. Even your mother knows."

"I doubt that. She lives five states away. I doubt she knows what her 25-year-old son did last night—"

"She knows."

Frank got quiet. Really quiet. Then he said, "How would she know? The cops only found out a few minutes ago."

"She has ESPM."

"You don't even know her. You haven't even been to her house. How do you know she has ESPN?"

"Not 'ESPN,' you idiot. 'ESPM.'"

"Oh. What's that?"

"Extra Sensory Perception of Mothers. Every mother has it."

"Well, my mother doesn't have it."

"Yes she does."

"No she doesn't."

"Fine. I'll prove it you, but first I want to make a bet with you."

"OK."

"I bet you five dollars that if you call her right now she will know A) that you played with a railroad track direction thingy and turned it the wrong way; and B) that you are calling her from a train right now cuz you're on the lam."

"I am not on the lam."

"Yes you are. You are on the lam from our friends and from the police."

"OK, so we didn't show up with the keg at the party Saturday like we promised. And there was a giant ruckus at the train depot Sunday afternoon. And we didn't come to school Monday morning. What makes you think everyone is going to tie all that to us?"

"Trust me—everyone, including your mother, is going to tie those three things together."

"My mother knows all this? Five bucks?"

"Five bucks."

"You're on. Before I call her, though, uh, which station are we getting off at again?"

Light from Below4 (ArtBloq: Trees, TreeArt)

Light from Below4

[(bill-holtsnider.pixels.com/featured/light-from-below4-bill-holtsnider.html)](bill-holtsnider.pixels.com/featured/light-from-below4-bill-holtsnider.html)

32. Two guys smoking behind the school

"So when and where is all this activity going to take place?"

"At the usual spot. At midnight."

"How mysterious. How secretive. How exotic. And just how are you going to get her there?"

"I have my ways."

"You have your 'ways'! Hah! You don't have a way out of this one stoplight town without GPS. Without a guide to hold your hand while you wander around, crying—"

"Are you finished?"

"Not yet. While you were crying, your Mom—"

"Leave my mother out of it."

"How 'bout your girlfriend, can I put her in it? Or should I say your 'imaginary girlfriend,' since none of us have ever seen her?"

"Like I would ever introduce her to you."

"Like she even exists."

"Oh, she exists, all right. Believe you me."

"'Believe you me'! What are you—from the 1940's? No one says that anymore."

"Just because you got an 'A' in Astronomy doesn't mean you can dis my language."

"Yes, as a matter of fact, yes it does."

"Or my girlfriend, either."

"Yes, her too. None of us have ever seen your girlfriend, we assume you have a mom only because you are here, and you speak like you are from some other time in history. Are you sure you aren't from another planet? Maybe Pluto, or Jupiter, or some exoplanet?"

"Exoplanets are not inhabited."

"Not by anything we can see yet, but they might contain life forms—"

"I am from Detroit, okay? I was born 16 years ago. My dad worked in a car factory and my mom—"

"Enough. I was right, you ARE from another planet. You're from Detroit."

"But unlike you, at least I am an intelligent life form."

Back in the Day (ArtBloq: Trees, TreeArt)

Back in the Day

(bill-holtsnider.pixels.com/featured/back-in-the-day-bill-holtsnider.html)

33.Later at the chalet

So then I say to him, "John, we must turn back."

"Do you?"

"Do we what? No we didn't do it—"

"Do you turn back?"

"Oh, yeah. We turned back."

"But do you make it all the way back?"

"Of course, man. I am here, aren't I?"

"Just because you are here doesn't mean you made it all the way back by yourselves."

"Well, I didn't say *by ourselves*."

Jerry smiled. "No, you're right, you did not say you made it back by yourselves. I take it that you got rescued."

"Well, we had help, let's put it that way."

"Like the city taxpayers helped that billionaire get his new football stadium."

"Exactly. He could have done it himself but he chose to get help."

"Might as well use OPM if you can get it."

"OPM?"

"'Other People's Money.'"

"Uh, yeah. Other People's Money."

"In your case, OPSP. Other People's Ski Patrol."

"Well, we *could* have made it down by ourselves, but we

chose not to."

"Because OPSP."

"No, because we thought it would be safer."

"It was. You guys could have died up there. You had no business being on a black diamond run."

"No, I don't mean us. We thought it would be safer for the Ski Patrol guys if we called them before we got into a tough spot. This way they could get us out safely instead of putting themselves at risk."

"Oh, I see. How kind and thoughtful of you."

"Yes, it was, wasn't it?"

Stump5 (ArtBloq: Trees, TreeArt)

Stump5

(bill-holtsnider.pixels.com/featured/stump5-bill-holtsnider.html)

34. Two girls in a dorm room the day after finals

"You are so hurtful. So vindictive."

"What do you mean?

"If I had a big, nasty secret, I sure wouldn't tell you."

"Why not?"

"Why would I? You never take anything I say seriously. You—"

"Do too. I took your rant on the 1880 Lincoln/Douglas debates—"

"1860."

"1860, 1880—who cares? I took your rant so seriously I wrote my English thesis on them."

"Hmmm. Those debates are famous for political and historical reasons, but I guess you could work their rhetorical characteristics into an English paper. Well, A PERSON could do that. I doubt YOU could do it."

"Ouch. For your information, Miss Smarty English Major, I got an 'A.'"

"Wow. The plagiarism filter must have been broken that day."

"I did not download it from the Internet, okay?"

"Whatever. You did not write an essay for English that was graded an 'A.' Didn't happen."

"Did too."

"Did not. Did your mother write it for you?"

"No."

"Your brother?"

"No."

"Did Mr. Gordon C. Bellweather give his prettiest student an 'A' for trying so hard?"

"Whatever do you mean?"

"You know exactly what I mean. Quid pro quo."

"Well, I don't know what that means, but I do know we both left his office yesterday with smiles on our faces..."

Bridge 32016 (ArtBloq: Bridges, BridgeArt)

Bridge 32016

(bill-holtsnider.pixels.com/featured/cubular-lake-and-clouds1-bill-holtsnider.html)

35. Two guys sitting in a bar discussing which planet they are from

"I am not sure you are even from this planet."

"Earth?"

"Yes, 'Earth.' You sound unsure."

"Well, if I was from another planet, I probably wouldn't tell anyone. Least of all you."

"Why not me? I'm your best friend. I would tell you if I was from another planet."

"No you wouldn't. Ah, that's it, I can see it now! You ARE from another planet. The whole thing fell in to our solar system from outer space."

Gerry looked at his friend for a second.

"OK, you got me," he said. "I am from planet StupidRock. How did you know?"

"Your haircut, for one—it makes Jerry Lewis look smart."

"Who?"

"Your deep grasp of culture, for another. You know what the Kardashians had for breakfast but you don't know who the Vice President is."

"Who is it?"

"Your clothes are another clue. You look like one of the Marx Brothers dressed you."

"TJ Maxx Brothers? Who are they?"

"I think the real clue to your origins, though, is your brother."

"Tearon."

"Yeah, that wizard. 40 years old and he still lives with his parents."

"Well, I am thinking of moving back in with Mom and Dad myself, for your information."

"Of course you are. But let's get back to the topic at hand. You are from another planet. And you have come—"

"To steal your women. We are here to repopulate our race and we need some women to help us with the breeding."

"Of course. But anyone from a place called StupidRock is going to have to break a few rules."

"Rules. Like what rules?"

"Like the rule about admitting where you are from. Lie. When you meet women and start dating, lie to them. Tell them you are from someplace exotic like Biloxi."

"Where's that?"

"It is the next planet over from StupidRock."

Summer Leaves2 (ArtBloq: Bridges, BridgeArt)

Summer Leaves2

(bill-holtsnider.pixels.com/featured/the-summer-leaves-bill-holtsnider.html)

36. Two brothers in their beds late at night

"So she takes your sword right out of your hand, just like that?"

"Yeah, just like that."

"And then what? Did you slap her?"

"Slap her?! She's my fencing instructor, for crying out loud. My ADVANCED FENCING CLASS instructor!"

"She schooled you just then, that is for sure."

"Well, she is supposed to be schooling me. That is her job."

"No, her job is to teach you how to fence. She is schooling you big time, my brother, but in the School of Love. Not the School of Fencing Things with Pointy Ends."

"No she is not."

"Yes she is."

"When did you come up with such a lame idea, anyway?"

"Well, for one thing, I have seen you two together."

"When you came to my lesson that time?"

"Yes. I saw how she looks at you."

"And for another thing?"

"I hear the way you talk about her."

"You're reading a whole lot into some small things. And for one thing, she is the same age as Mother. The two knew each other back in college."

"So?"

"So who wants a girlfriend twenty years older than he is?"

"You said the word 'girlfriend,' I did not."

"I said I did not want a—"

"As if you had a choice."

"I do have a choice and I am going to make it. I am going over to MaryBeth's house one more time."

"It'll be the last time."

"You don't know that."

"Yes I do. That girl is pretty, about your age, has no boyfriend, stays out late on Friday and Saturday night partying. She is perfect for you. Except for one thing—she can't stand you."

"I'm going to fix that."

"With what—plastic surgery and a complete personality transplant? Oh, and by the way, her house is ten times bigger and nicer than ours. Her little mansion. Our whole house could fit in her driveway—hell, it could probably fit in her garage. So you had better rob a few banks on your way over to propose to her."

"I am not proposing to her—yet."

"Look, as your older brother let me make a couple of small suggestions."

"If you must."

"I must. One, forget MaryBeth. She has forgotten you more

times than you look at that picture of her on your phone."

"You know about that?"

"Of course I know about that. Everyone has seen you mooning like a schoolgirl at your phone. Since you don't have any friends, you can't be looking at texts from them."

"Ouch."

"What are brothers for except to say stuff like this? And two, chase the fencing lady down. See if you can get your sword back. So to speak."

Across the Black3 (ArtBloq: Bridges, BridgeArt)

Across the Black3

(bill-holtsnider.pixels.com/featured/across-the-black3-bill-holtsnider.html)

37.Two men in a jail visiting room

"Is there a reason you think that? I mean, besides the fact that you are incredibly stupid?"

"So YOU say."

"No, no—I don't want to claim all the credit. I think most people who meet you are impressed by how stupid you are."

"At least they are impressed."

"Yes, they are impressed. They thought there was a bar that no one could be lower than for stupidity, but you, my friend, shock them. You are stupider than stupid."

"Well, at least I am not meaner than mean."

"I ain't mean, bro, I am just telling it like it is."

"Sometimes that is mean. It is very mean."

"Sometimes the truth hurts."

"Well, sometimes it doesn't HAVE to."

"Yes it does. I am a truth teller, my friend. I tell the truth come hell or higher, higher water."

"Telling the truth is not always the right thing to do."

"What are you talking about?! OF COURSE it is always the right thing to do. I thought you were a Catholic—you're not suggesting I lie, are you?" Benito smiled as he said that, letting the phrase hang over the conversation like an iguana in the afternoon sun.

"I AM suggesting that sometimes not telling the truth—"

"Lying."

"Lying—sometimes lying is better than telling the truth."

"As if. I can't believe you—Mr. Goody Two Shoes—are saying this. Give me one example."

"Well, remember that time last week when you got those speeding tickets?"

"Like I could forget. I have been driving that road for over 10 years and have never seen a cop there. Suddenly, I get pulled over twice in one day."

"If you had told the second officer you had already been arrested once that day—"

"He would have let me off scot free? Ha! As if! How was I supposed to know those guys had computers where they could check who got arrested that day?"

"Everyone has computers today. Even *I* have a computer and I can't even type."

"Even YOU have a computer and you're not the type."

"Well, at least I am not in jail, asking my best friend for bail to get me out."

"You're not my best friend."

"Best friend, only friend, whatever. Oh, look, it appears I forgot my wallet..."

Ring of Clouds (ArtBloq: Clouds, CloudArt)

Ring of Clouds

(bill-holtsnider.pixels.com/featured/ring-of-clouds-bill-holtsnider.html)

38. Two working women in the back of a police squad car

"I told you not to wear the red halter dress. There's attention and then there's *attention*."

"I am sooo tired of you telling me after the fact what we should have done and not done. We both make our living lying on our backs, Marcia, and that is the basic fact. Spittle happens."

"Spittle happens! Spittle happens! Is that the best you can do?"

"What do you mean, 'Is that the best I can do?' What do you want me to do—call your mother?"

"Someone has to call her and it ain't gonna be me."

"Well, I am not calling her."

"Yes you are."

"No I am not."

"She's your mother, too."

"So what? We have been through this a hundred times. You and I fight, I am the one who ends up calling her, I listen to the same old tired stories about how she had such high hopes for us sisters back when we were in first grade in Indiana, then our father left, blah, blah, blah. I could recite all the stories word-for-word for her."

Marcia was not listening. Her sister rambled on but Marcia

was zoned out by the blue and red lights of the squad car, hypnotized by the rhythm.

"Marcia! Marcia? Are you listening to me?!"

"Huh? Oh, uh, what? Yeah, sure, whatever. I'll pay the fee."

"Of course you'll pay the fee. That is the LEAST of our worries."

"What do you mean?"

"What do I mean? What do I mean?! Do you think for one minute those lazy-ass husbands of ours are going to stay married to us after this? After we get arrested?!"

"Larry loves me."

"Larry loves money, honey, not you. He is not a manager of the seventh-largest hedge fund in the country because he loves you. He loves money."

"He loves me. He told me himself."

Her sister snorted. "You make your money lying on your back on a bed with him, he makes his standing up in a networking meeting with other businessmen. But you're both in the same profession."

At that, Marcia burst out crying and her sister knew it was time to call their mother.

"Jam. That reminds me," the sister thought as the police sirens on the car blared around her and Marcia sobbed in the seat next to her, "I wonder if Momma has finished the canning for the fall yet?"

Across the Way3 (ArtBloq: Bridges, BridgeArt)

Across the Way3

[(bill-holtsnider.pixels.com/featured/across-the-way3-bill-holtsnider.html)](bill-holtsnider.pixels.com/featured/across-the-way3-bill-holtsnider.html)

39. Two brothers sitting in a tractor that had crashed into the barn

"Well, now what?"

"What're ya looking at me for? It was your idea to come here. You're the one who wanted to go for a ride. A 'joyride' I think you called it."

"Just because it was my idea doesn't mean you had to go along with it."

"Yes it does. You come up with the ideas and I do them. I put 'em into action. Only this one didn't work out so well."

"Me crashing Daddy's new two-hundred-thousand-dollar tractor into Ted's barn? No, that idea did not work out so well."

"We can't back up."

"Or go forward."

"And Ted's chickens are loose."

"And his two horses are wandering around."

"And one pig, maybe two, got crushed."

"And the front blade got bent."

"And the transmission appears shot."

"These things have transmissions?"

"If you had not run away to college you'd know all our tractors have 4-wheel-drive transmissions."

"I did not run away to college, I *left* for college. You, Dad, Mom—you guys knew all the way through high school I was going to go to college. Why you were so surprised when I got accepted and then left for Mizzou is still a mystery to me."

"I know you told me and all, but we didn't expect you to actually go. I expected you to stay and work on the farm with me. Dad and Mom can't do it all themselves like they used to, you know."

"Yes, I know that. But I was never going to stay here. This farm, this town—hell, this whole state—drives me nuts. I was going crazy here! You know that."

His brother looked down sadly at wreckage.

"Yeah, well," he said brightly, "at least the radio still works."

"There's that."

Kokopellilike Bird7 (ArtBloq: Mixed Drawings on Photos)

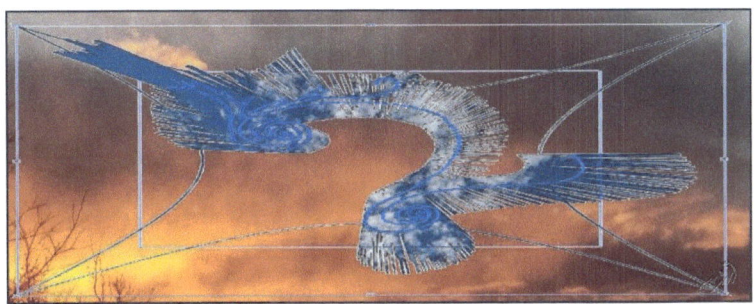

Kokopellilike Bird7

(bill-holtsnider.pixels.com/featured/kokopelli-like-bird7-bill-holtsnider.html)

40. Three rich manboys at a coffee shop

"I can't find my way out of this Starbucks, that's how bad my sense of direction is," said Stan, smiling.

"You say that like it's a good thing."

"Isn't being trapped in a place with all the coffee you can drink a good thing?"

"'All the coffee you can drink' and 'All the coffee you can afford' are two different things."

"Your daddy can afford all the coffee you can drink."

"Let's leave my daddy out of this, shall we?" said Stan.

"Uh oh, somebody's touchy about the checks he gets every month."

"I AM touchy about those checks. I wish I didn't need them, but I do."

The other guys nodded. "Yeah, we get those checks and we wish we didn't need 'em and we desperately need 'em," said Dan.

"So what should we do?"

"What should we do to stop getting those checks?"

"We have been over this hundreds of times. Let's face it—we have no skills."

"We have the skill of being the sons of very rich men."

"Which is harder to do than it looks, by the way."

"As if. How is getting a five thousand dollar check in the

mail every month hard to do?"

"Well, somebody has to get it from the mailbox, take it to the bank, put it in the bank…"

"You're serious, aren't you?"

"Of course I am serious. Not every Joe Blow can do that."

"Can too."

"Well, not every Jane Blow can do it, how about that?"

"Leave Jane Blow out of this. You and Jane Blodine are done. That relationship is kaput."

"You don't have to get all negative on me."

"Yes I do. You bring that woman up every time we talk about something. We are talking about money and banks and you bring her into the conversation. If we were talking about spaceships, you'd find a way to work in a mention of Jane Bleepin' Blodine."

"I miss her."

"I know you do. But for the record, no one else does…"

Green Floating Mamba (ArtBloq: Mixed Drawings on Photos)

Green Floating Mamba

(bill-holtsnider.pixels.com/featured/green-floating-mamba-bill-holtsnider.html)

41.Two men in a stateroom before the big breakup

"And then what?"

"And then what what?"

"You know what I mean. After the ship hits the fan and all the shouting starts, then what?"

"I laugh."

"That's it? You laugh?"

"Yes, I laugh."

"You laugh your way to prison."

"Maybe, but probably not. I don't think McClure will do anything."

"Are you kidding me? Let me get this straight: your plan is to throw his five thousand dollar model ship into the cooling fan in front of him and all his family."

"Yes."

"You don't think he'll do anything? Ha! He'll sue you so fast the ink on the lawsuit will blur."

"No he won't."

"'No he won't'? Are you crazy? He'd sue his own family if he thought he could get five dollars from them."

"Precisely."

"What does that mean?"

"It means they know—because I told them—that it is not his model ship. It is mine."

"As if."

"It IS mine. I made it last year. I studied the designs, I bought the materials, I built it. It took me six months, working every single night. He broke into my cabin the night after I finished it and stole it. He has been telling people ever since that it's his ship."

"Why didn't you tell me that before?"

"When the model hits the fan and breaks into a million pieces, all the innards of the model will spill out on the floor and the secret note I tucked in there will tumble out, too."

"What'd you write on the note?"

"'My nickname is Moron McClure. I can't glue two popsicle sticks together. So I could not and did not make this model.'"

"Oh. Nice. I guess. Of course, once you smash it, he won't have it, but neither will you."

"Let's go back to that first part about him not having it, shall we?"

Swirlin'4 (ArtBloq: Mixed Drawings on Photos)

Swirlin'4

(http://bill-holtsnider.pixels.com/featured/swirlin4-bill-holtsnider.html)

42. Three men sitting in an office before the heist

"So when do we go?"

"Jay and I are leaving in a few hours."

Terman looked at him for a minute and then stormed out of the shop.

"That was harsh," Jay said.

"It wasn't harsher than it needed to be," I replied.

"He was with us from the beginning."

"No, he was with us IN NAME from the beginning. He wasn't doing any work, he was just stealing credit when he could, telling people how vital he was, putting his name on the letterhead."

"Since when do bank robbers have letterhead, anyway?"

"I told you, to be legitimate we have to look official. We have an office, we have a company car, we have a secretary—"

"I get the office and the car. And I can certainly see why you want Betty around. But stationery?"

"I've got my own business cards, too."

"What?! Why didn't you get me some?"

"You are not important enough to have a business card."

"WHAT?! Not important enough! The whole thing was my idea!"

"So what?"

"So what? Without me you guys would have nothing.

Nothing. Nada. The Big Belch-o."

"No, without ME you would have Belch-o. I executed all this. You helped, sure, but I was the one who made it happen."

"As if."

"As if yourself. You couldn't make breakfast happen if I gave you a menu and a twenty-dollar bill."

"Well, for your information, Mr. Everything, I am going to the police."

"Fine. Go to the police. Terman has already been there. But when they show up at my door and ask for my plans to break into the bank, I will show them this."

With that, I pulled out my stack of new printed business cards. They were on cream-colored stock with embossed, dark brown lettering. Everything was italicized but my name. And below my name was my title: "CPA, License to Steal..."

Thru the Trees (ArtBloq: Rivers, River Art)

Thru the Trees

[(bill-holtsnider.pixels.com/featured/thru-the-trees-bill-holtsnider.html)](bill-holtsnider.pixels.com/featured/thru-the-trees-bill-holtsnider.html)

43.A woman and her young son at breakfast

"I want a pet gorilla."

"Hmm."

"Did you hear what I said?"

"A pet. You want a pet. That's fine, dear. We'll get you a dog."

"Not a dog. A gorilla. I want a pet GORILLA!"

The mother put down her newspaper and looked at her son.

"Even if I wanted to, I couldn't get you a pet gorilla."

"I heard you yell at Daddy last night that you can do whatever you want, so I know you can get me a pet gorilla if you want to."

"No, I can't."

"Yes you can."

"No I can't. There is not enough room in this house, for one thing."

"This isn't a house, it's an apartment. And I don't want to live here anymore anyway. I want to move to a real house."

"Well, we might just do that, dear, very soon. Daddy is on an important business trip and when he gets back tomorrow we'll find out if we are going to move."

"Can we move into a real house?"

"Maybe. We'll have to see. It depends on where we are

going, what the terms of the relo package are—"

"What's a 'relo package'?"

"Oh, never mind that. But it matters to your father and it matters to me."

"Does a relo package have gorillas in it?"

"It can, honey, it definitely can. We had one once that had an 800-pound gorilla in it."

"Did it fit in the room?"

"Oh, it fit in the room. It was definitely there, though no one talked about it. But then it went away."

"Why? Why did it go away?"

"Because you came along, dear," the mother said, smiling at the memory. "Because you came along."

Not a Purple River (ArtBloq: Rivers, River Art)

Not a Purple River

(bill-holtsnider.pixels.com/featured/not-a-purple-river-bill-holtsnider.html)

44. Buying jet skis for the whole family

"Just how is this gonna save us money?"

Momma was worried. Very worried. In her mind they had no business bringing a family of five to the Everglades for a weeklong vacation. But Daddyo (his nickname for himself that no one else used except ironically) insisted. After months of bickering, she finally gave in. But the first day they got here he insisted on buying the whole family jet skis. Not renting them, mind you, which is what every other self-respecting family would do. No, he had to buy them. One for each of them.

Naturally, the salesman in the motor sports store was thrilled. He had offered them a series of "special deals" that he "personally negotiated with the manager." "Ron" had become a dear, dear friend who would do anything for the family. Anything. He had repeated this often in the thirty-five minutes they had known him.

"Don't worry, Momma, we'll be fine. We need these jet skis this week and we'll need them every time we come back down here."

"IF we ever come back down here."

"WHEN we come back down here."

"Momma—may I call you Momma?" Ron began.

"NO!" the married couple shouted in unison.

"Ron, stick to talking about the machines, son. Don't spend

time being so familiar," said Daddyo.

"Yes, please get to the point. How much will it cost us to buy five jet skis from you today?" Momma's patience was wearing thin.

"If you buy five jet skis today I can have them delivered to you next month for—"

"NEXT MONTH?!" they both shouted at him at once.

"Yes, well, at the moment all our machines are being used for rentals. We will have to order from the factory in Michigan—"

Momma turned and walked out of the store. The three kids followed her. Daddyo was left in the showroom. Ron saw his fabulous five-jet-ski sale disappear right before his eyes.

"June is our most popular month, and—" Ron said.

Before he could finish, Daddyo looked at him sadly, thinking of all the mountains he had climbed, the alligators he had fought, to get to the final moment, and then this happened. "Son, we will never see you, your store, or your manager again. And I can't say it has been fun."

Lazy River 5 (ArtBloq: Rivers, River Art)

Lazy River 5

[*(bill-holtsnider.pixels.com/featured/lazy-river5-bill-holtsnider.html)*](bill-holtsnider.pixels.com/featured/lazy-river5-bill-holtsnider.html)

45. They had just gotten off the boat

"THIS is it? THIS is what we fought so hard to get to?"

"You can't judge a book by its cover. Just like you can't judge a city by its ports."

"Save me the clichés. We worked like dogs to get here and now all I see are shipping containers."

"Yes, shipping containers full of the gold you and I will make once we get our business up and going."

"Shipping containers full of crap is more like it. I want to go back."

"Well, that is not really possible, dearest."

"Why not? You said we could come to the city and look around. If we don't like it, we go back."

"Yes, well, I did say that, but it is not technically true. Not anymore, anyway."

"What exactly does that mean?!"

He could feel the cold fury building behind those green eyes. "Well, dear, it means—"

"Don't you 'Well dear' me, buster. Get to the point: can we go back or not?"

"Not."

She looked at the boat as it slowly sailed away. "And why not, may I ask?"

"Well, as you can see, our ship has sailed. Literally and

metaphorically."

"You brought me all the way here to make a joke? You think this is funny?!"

"Hardly. But when I said we could 'try it and come back if we don't like it,' that was before your mother—"

"My mother! My mother? What does she have to do with it?"

"That was before she told me that I was a worthless, no-good frog that was too useless for her daughter. After ten years of marriage she still hates me."

"Yes, she does. And maybe she is right—maybe you are too useless for me."

"Well, then she said that if I divorced you, she would pay me $50,000."

"What?!"

"And if I did NOT divorce you, she would no longer send us the allowance she mails us every month."

"Let me get this straight: You turned down fifty thousand bucks to stay married to me?"

"Yes."

"And now we have no more money from her coming in to live on?"

"Yes."

"She's right, you are useless."

Silver River (ArtBloq: Rivers, River Art)

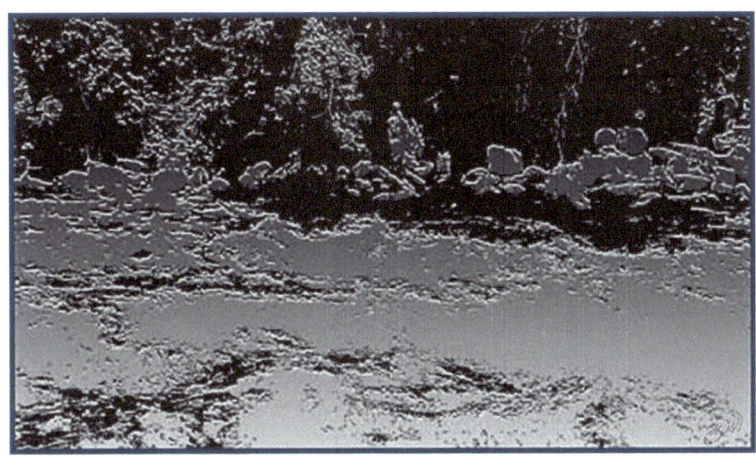

Silver River

[*(bill-holtsnider.pixels.com/featured/silver-river-bill-holtsnider.html)*](bill-holtsnider.pixels.com/featured/silver-river-bill-holtsnider.html)

46. Two guys talking about kids

"And the bear tried to climb in through the window."

"Was it a girl?"

"A girl?! I didn't check, but what difference would that have made?"

"You could have serenaded her."

"What? What are you talking about?"

Bert began singing, "She came in through the bathroom window –."

"Yeah, right. You ARE old."

"Whoa! I am not that old. 19 is not old."

"Compared to your 2-year old brother you are."

"So? He's way young."

"And you are way old."

"My mom is the old one. Imagine having a child at 41."

"I am a guy, I cannot even imagine having a child, no matter what age we are talking about."

"Do you ever think about having kids?"

"What part of 'I-am-a-guy' did you not understand?"

"You think being a guy means you can't want kids? YOU are the old one, dude."

Forked River (ArtBloq: Rivers, River Art)

Forked River

[(bill-holtsnider.pixels.com/featured/forked-river1-bill-holtsnider.html)](bill-holtsnider.pixels.com/featured/forked-river1-bill-holtsnider.html)

47.A group on some kind of boat

"Are we going to jump in, or are we just going to stand here and talk about jumping in?"

"I am in favor of just standing here and *talking about* starting."

"Of course you are. You are never in favor of DOING anything, you're just in favor of APPEARING to do something. You are in favor of just TALKING ABOUT doing something. Not ACTUALLY doing it."

Everyone at the table shifted uncomfortably in their seats. Dan D. and Danny D. had just gotten divorced. And neither wanted to leave the startup they just worked for, though their friends had counseled them repeatedly that one of them should do it and do it quickly.

"Look, you two," said Marnie, the boss. "I said nothing when you guys kept your stupidly similar names when you joined our group. I said nothing when you guys joined at the same time. I said nothing when you wanted to travel to the convention and stay in the same room, which was against company policy, by the way. But I am saying something now: any more of this kind of petty bickering and you are both off the project. Off. Done."

An uncomfortable silence filled the room.

Finally, Marnie began to speak again. "Now that we are

clear on that point—"

"Excuse me, boss."

"Yes, Mark, what is it? What do you think we should do?"

"I think we should jump in. Now. Right this minute."

Of course he would say that, thought Marnie, he would be for jumping in regardless of the costs. "And why do you think the best course of action is for seven inexperienced trekkers to jump into an icy river?"

"Icy river? Oh, I thought the question was 'Should we jump on a phone call to ask for help from the helicopter guide that brought us here?'"

Everyone else at the table laughed.

"No, that is not the question, Mark. Do you still think we should jump in to the natural soft drink market, which is a new market for us, right now?"

"No, not really."

More laughter.

"Just because our former CEO reminded us all the time that he used to be a helicopter pilot and just because he got the company into sales markets outside its core competency doesn't mean we HAVE to get into the natural soft drink market. We could stay in craft beer market and do just fine."

Terrera spoke up. "Except for Schumpeter, of course."

"Yeah, except for him."

The Path Upward2 tshirt (ArtBloq: T-shirt Designs)

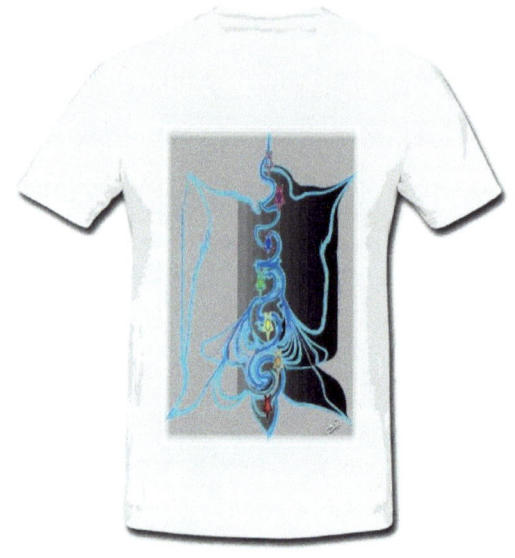

The Path Upward2 tshirt1

(bill-holtsnider.pixels.com/products/the-path-upwards-bill-holtsnider-adult-tshirt.html)

48. Flying solo for the first time

"So precisely what is required to do this again?"

"You're kidding, right?"

"No I am not kidding. I don't know what we need to do next."

"Panic. I vote we panic next."

"Relax, it will be fine. I just need to get my sea legs under me."

"You need to get your sea legs under you?"

"Yeah."

"At 35,000 feet in the air?"

"Well, yeah. I thought I remembered but I don't."

"It's like riding a bicycle, for crying out loud."

"No it's not."

"It totally is. Just start pedaling."

"Easy for you to say. You're already married."

"Relax. You've already done the hard part—you found the girl. Now just make it official."

"By going to a wedding."

"By going to the wedding you and your bride are having up here in this plane. In the sky. In an airplane. That could crash."

"The plane is not going to crash."

"Easy for you to say. You're both pilots. The rest of us are just passengers on the airplane of life."

"Now you're getting sentimental and maudlin."

"Maudlin?"

"Sad. Mopey. Depressing. The Big Downer. Sucka—"

"OK, OK—I get it. Now just go out there and walk down the aisle, please."

"Nah, I've changed my mind. I don't want to get married after all."

"Good, because I wanted to try out these tandem parachutes. So when I go out there and tell Marnie that you changed your mind and no longer want to marry her, at 35,000 feet or no feet, she is going to throw me out of the plane."

"She will, but at least you'll have the chute. When she throws me out, I'll be flying commando."

waves t-shirt (ArtBloq: T-shirt Designs)

waves t-shirt

[_(bill-holtsnider.pixels.com/products/waves1-bill-holtsnider-adult-tshirt.html)_](bill-holtsnider.pixels.com/products/waves1-bill-holtsnider-adult-tshirt.html)

49. Under the trellis during the wedding ceremony for the recently arrived

Bride: "And?"

Groom: "And that means we are friends forever."

Bride: "So does that mean we go on vacations together?"

Groom: "Yes."

Bride: "And share a bathtub?"

Groom: "Uh, yes. Although I draw the line at sharing razors."

The Minister Pronouncer Guy: "I now pronounce you—"

Bride: "Wait! Don't pronounce yet!"

Groom: "Yeah, don't pronounce yet. Wait, uh, why not?"

Bride: "Because I am not finished."

Groom: "You're not finished with what?"

Bride: "Finished asking questions. I still have some things I need to know."

The Minister Pronouncer Guy: "Young lady, the wedding ceremony is not the place to ask questions, if I may say so—"

The Bride and the Groom: "YOU MAY NOT!!"

Groom: "Go ahead. Keep asking."

Bride: "Thank you. Do you have any pets?"

The Wedding Pronouncer Guy looked away. He did not want his face to give his amusement away. He had agreed to be the officiant at the "Weddings For People Who Just Met On The

Flight Out Here" as a favor to a friend. He never thought he would actually have to do one of these ceremonies, yet here he was.

Groom: "No."

Bride: "Oh, that is a bummer."

Groom: "Because you have a pet?"

Bride: "Because I have several pets."

Groom: "Oh, that's okay. I love dogs. And I can stand cats. Barely, but I can stand them."

Bride: "Uh, can you stand snakes and ferrets?"

SangyFroidal t-shirt (ArtBloq: T-shirt Designs)

SangyFroidal t-shirt

(www.bill-holtsnider.pixels.com/T-shirt Designs/SangyFroidal t-shirt.jpg)

50.Stuff at the End

Note on Originality

All the conversations in this book are entirely fictional. I made them up. All the art in this book was created entirely by me.

Dedication

For the far flung four, and the other far flung four. Please be safe. And to The Fam; without you I could not have done this. You are my everything.

Acknowledgements

A special thx to all those folks at the BWA, an org that has helped me for a long time with all the facets of The Writing. Muchas gracias. And thx to my editor, ML, for making this a more correct document.

A Note about Creating the Graphics

The art was created digitally. In most cases it began in the "real world" as a hand drawing or a photograph but was converted and then modified digitally. I used Adobe Creative Suite (primarily Illustrator, though Photoshop and After Effects were also brought into play), SnagIt, and Microsoft Word (which has more graphic editing tools than you might expect). Enjoy!

Other Books

Coming out Later in 2016

- One Page Conversations, Vol. 2: Some Words and Some Art (November, 2016)

Coming in 2017

- Nanomaplings: Some Possible Maps of the Mind/Brain, a (fictional) treatise of a book of diagrams accompanied by descriptions of (hitherto) undiscovered functions of the Mind/Brain
- Some Rivers Run: Five Stories from the Frontier (short stories)

Previously Published

- IT Manager's Handbook: Getting your New Job Done, 3rd (2012) by Bill Holtsnider and Brian D. Jaffe (amazon link)
- Pocket Guide To Hiring Geeks (2012) by Bill Holtsnider and George Stragand (amazon link)
- Agile Development and Business Goals: The Six Week Solution (2010) by Bill Holtsnider, Tom Wheeler, Joe Gee and George Stragand (amazon link)
- IT Manager's Handbook: The Business Edition (2009) by Bill Holtsnider and Brian D. Jaffe (amazon link)
- IT Manager's Handbook: Getting your New Job Done, 2nd (2006) by Bill Holtsnider and Brian D. Jaffe (amazon link)
- IT Manager's Handbook: Getting your new job done,1st (2000) by Bill Holtsnider and Brian D. Jaffe (amazon link)
- Windows 98 Step by Step: A Hands-On-Guide (1998) by Bill Holtsnider (amazon link)
- Windows 95 Step by Step: A Hands-On Workbook (1997) by Bill Holtsnider (amazon link)

Thank you for reading my latest book. The next volume of this series will be out in October, 2016.